I0684265

Copyright © by Teri N. Tenaglia

March 2018

ISBN: 978-0999356418

Prologue

Dreams are one of those topics that intrigue people. Everyone has them, they are not controllable, and they have different levels of meaning according to Freud. If a third of a lifespan is spent asleep, that suggests a psychological significance to these subconscious manifestations. Some parts of dreams are considered residual, merely leftover fragments of daily occurrences. More emotional dreams are said to be recalls of flash bulb memories, which are significant snipits from a wheelhouse of special moments. Nightmares are negative configurations of altered fragments rearranged into the disillusioning, disturbing, and bizarre. The unpredictability of dreams makes them equally intriguing and mysterious. On very rare occasions, dreams have the ability to wake people up, make a memory resurface, Alter a mood, and sometimes communicate information or create an awareness. The dreamer is usually left confused to ponder the meaning and why it happened.

Dreams are the playground of the subconscious where people are most vulnerable. They can conjure any sense—a smell, sound, touch, feeling, image—and recreate all emotions. Not everyone remembers their dreams, but they have them every night. Some individuals are able to wake up during a dream and return to it, while others are paralyzed by them. Most confounding of all is when a dream seems to wield itself into reality. Then they earn the title of premonition. Given the sorted nature of dreams and vast array of symbolism they can employ, they make understanding the experience of a premonition extremely difficult. Since timing is typically a critical factor in determining the proper course of action, this intensifies the urgency to act on what has been shown to the dreamer, yet still never really answer the question why. What follows are some of those examples that forced their way into reality yet cannot be explained.

The Cafeteria

Shooting up from a restless sleep, drenched in a cold sweat, Toni grabbed for the phone at her bedside and called her principal without hesitation. She never even looked at the clock. It was dark outside, even for Spring. After five rings a sleepy voice answered, "Hello?"

"Ralph, it's Toni. I'm sorry to wake you. I have to tell you something," she said with urgency in her voice still out of breath and disturbed by her dream.

"It's 4:30 in the morning. Did you even go to sleep yet? 'Cause I know there's no way you got up early. What's so important?" he said with a long yawn.

"You have to block off the left section of the cafeteria today, the part by the glass. You can't let kids sit there. If they do, they're going to get hurt," Toni said with a serious tone.

"Tone, we barely have enough room in the cafeteria with the school under renovations. There's nowhere to put the kids we have. We're already sitting way too many at a table as it is. Why do you think the kids are going to get hurt? What's wrong?" He searched for some logic.

"Ralph, it's going to sound weird, but you know me really well, and I always tell you exactly what I think."

"That would be an understatement," he said sarcastically.

"I dreamt that we were at lunch duty today, and toward the end of the last lunch a

2

few of the men working on the roof outside on the extension fell and lost control of one of the steel girders. It flew pendulum style right through the glass into the cafeteria and killed the students sitting at the booths. There was blood everywhere. Lots of students were hurt. Everyone was screaming. It was so disturbing; it woke me up."

"You woke me up at 4:30 in the morning on a Friday to tell me about a dream?" he said like he had just heard a bad joke.

"It wasn't just a dream. It was one of those dreams. I can't explain it," she sounded concerned.

"It's a dream! I'm sure it seemed real, but you woke up and it wasn't!"

"You don't get it. Every now and again I have these strange dreams that happen. They're not always exactly like the dream, but they're close, like some object may substitute for something in reality but they always happen right afterward. I dream all the time no differently than anyone else, but rarely I'll have one of these dreams. I can't explain how I know. I just do. They feel weird and I get an icky feeling. I wanted to tell you before school started so that you could shut down that section to keep the kids safe," she said with conviction.

"You're crazy! I can't shut down that section on a dream! Go back to bed. I'll see you in a couple hours," he said as he hung up the phone. Toni sank back in her bed defeated. She couldn't go back to sleep. Images of the dream kept playing like a bad loop tape in her mind.

Toni was usually sprinting in the door at 7:29, but today she was in the parking lot by 6:50. She went about her usual routine, checking her mailbox, greeting colleagues, and getting ready for her first class, but she was preoccupied. Her every thought was fixated on

4

the image of that girder crashing through the window. Her students entered her classroom and interrupted her awful thought.

"Hola! Happy Friday! Do you want me to change the calendar?" an enthusiastic student asked while picking up the container that held the calendar magnets.

About a minute elapsed before Toni realized she hadn't responded. She looked up from her blank stare and nodded, "That would be fantastic, Paco. Gracias!" She made a conscious effort to seem like nothing was wrong, but it was obvious.

Class by class passed as Toni explained conjugations on the whiteboard while thinking about which of her students sat in those dreaded seats during lunch. Her classes ended and she was finished teaching for the day. "Just get through lunch duty, prep for Monday, and go home. That's all you have to do. Don't think about it. Just do it," she was talking to herself as the French teacher opened the classroom door.

"You talking to yourself again?" She didn't seem surprised.

"You caught me, Claire. Me talking to myself is pretty typical," she said with a weak smile trying to seem normal.

"Did your self answer?"

"I did. I'm a little twitchy today," Toni admitted.

"I see that. What's up?" she asked in the kindly way she has.

"I had one of *those* dreams. It really bothered me. It bugged me so much I woke Ralph up at 4:30 to tell him about it," she said as if that was standard.

"You woke Ralph up? Why? What was this one about that you felt the need to call him

6

at that hour?" Claire asked as she walked toward her.

"I dreamt that the guys working on the roof fell, a steel girder got loose, and crashed through the glass into the cafeteria hurting a lot of kids. Some even got killed. It was bad. Woke me up. I couldn't breathe. I asked Ralph to close that section."

"How did he react?" she asked genuinely interested.

"He thinks I'm loca. I'm worried about this one," she said as she looked up for advice.

"Well, he doesn't know about the others, and you must admit this is very different," she looked over her glasses waiting for confirmation.

"It's very different. This one is scary. I better get down there." She glanced at the clock on the wall. "If it's going to happen, this is

7

the lunch that it does," she said opening the door to leave.

"You're super early though," Claire said calmly.

"I'm super paranoid!" Toni said while raising an eyebrow.

"Nothing new there. I'll see you at eighth. Hopefully nothing will happen. Good luck!" she raised her already incredibly loud volume so Toni would hear.

The door opened again a few seconds later, "Merci, Frenchy! If I can't get Ralph to listen to me, maybe I can get the kids to. It's no accident students love their foreign language teachers. We're quirky!" She exited again.

"You got that right!" Claire unnecessarily raised her voice a second time.

Toni walked down to the cafeteria focused on only one thought—could she get her boss to move the kids and close off the section by the glass? When she arrived, the students were just arriving to the hot lunch and snack lines. She scanned the crowd for her principal, who, other than currently thinking she was insane, was a good-natured, funny, blond man. He walked in and she immediately rushed to plead her case again. "Ralph, I know you think I'm bananas, but this is the lunch! Let's move the kids just in case. If nothing happens— great!"

He rolled his eyes, "Tone, nothing's gonna happen! You have to stop worrying about this. It was a dream—a bad dream. I get it, but we don't even have anywhere to put these kids now. Look. The construction dudes are fine. They know what they're doing. I wish they'd do it faster, because I feel like we've been under construction forever, but they've got it under control," he assured her.

She looked at the students by the window, now eating their lunch, some waving

9

at the construction people and watching them work. "I hope you're right, but I've had dreams like this before, and they happen. It's not always exactly the same way, but they do. You just have to trust me," her face was begging him to reconsider.

"Relax! I know it seemed real. Dreams can really shake you up. You know what I always say—be a cow. Know what a cow does in the rain?" he waited as if his proverb would suddenly make sense. "Nothing. They just stand there, so be a cow. It'll be okay." He smiled and walked toward the Friday pizza menu.

"*Someday I hope that equates to something important, some gem of wisdom that isn't totally weird*," Toni thought to herself. She paced the length of the glass side of the cafeteria relentlessly. Every so many students, she'd stop and say hi as an excuse to look at the construction workers. Nothing unusual seemed to be happening. Eventually, the last lunch period was over and it was time to dismiss the students. Ralph could see her anxiety, so he released the section by the glass first. They made their way toward the door. It felt like an eternity to Toni, who watched the construction workers and students exiting like a tennis match. The process took a while, since there were in excess of 350 students who needed to leave the cafeteria by sections. Finally, the last forty or so students stood up to leave. Ralph walked toward the center of the cafeteria, where Toni met him. He put his arm around her and said, "See? I told you everything was gonna be okay. Nothing happened. The kids are all safe---"Ralph was interrupted by a booming metallic sound. The remaining students and teachers turned to see where the noise came from, and looked out the giant windows just in time to see a construction man lying on the makeshift roof of the new addition surrounded by a group of men in hard hats. There was lots of commotion and loud voices could be heard from outside. One of the men grabbed for a walkie talkie on his belt, when another shouted, "Look out! It's gonna hit!" At that moment a huge, red, steel girder hanging by a rope attached to a crane on top of the next building picked up momentum and crashed through the wall of glass on the far side of the cafeteria. It hit like a freight train and glass shards flew everywhere. Larger panels from where it pierced the glass at the top fell like guillotines with jagged edges enough to slice anything in their path. The girder sailed through the cafeteria until it slammed into the cash register station with enough impact to bust open the drawers and send change flying among the glass on the floor. Students screamed, teachers gasped, the construction workers scrambled outside to prevent another girder from falling, and during the chaos, Toni stood frozen as if she was watching her own private movie. She'd watched this scene a mere few hours before. She turned to see the students, safe by the door. There was no noise or movement for a minute. Then Ralph touched Toni on the shoulder to get her attention. She looked at him as if to say, "*I warned you*." With a sullen look he whispered, "I'll never doubt you again." Then he took his cell phone off his belt clip and called the office for an ambulance and maintenance. The other teachers hurried the students out of the cafeteria to their next class. Toni's colleague, the French teacher, appeared, "Are you all right? The kids told me what happened."

"We're lucky the kids didn't get hurt," she said deflated and still in shock.

"It's not your fault. You tried to warn him," she reassured.

"Trying implies failure," Toni said matter of factly.

"Maybe once this calms down you should tell him about the other dreams too," she suggested earnestly.

"Maybe. I don't know if the others would matter now," she shrugged.

"I think they would, especially now. Come on. Let's go," she motioned toward the door as maintenance entered to clean up the glass. As they began sweeping, the two left the cafeteria in silence.

The Shuttle

A few weeks went by and the last days of school were nearing. One afternoon while she was looking over the yearbook distribution list, Ralph opened Toni's classroom door, poked his head in, and said, "Got a minute?" It seemed important.

"For the best boss in the world, anything. ¿Qué pasa?" she was being her usual, comical self.

"It's been a little while, but I haven't forgotten," he said seriously.

"About what?" she asked honestly, not knowing what he meant.

"Your dream about the cafeteria. How did you know that?" He pulled up a chair and sat down with his head on his hand as if waiting for a story like most people do in her classroom.

"I wish I had a better answer for you other than, `I just know,' but I don't. Every now and again I have a weird dream. They're very rare, but they happen, and when they do, they just feel weird. There's something more to them while I'm dreaming, then they wake me up. I guess that's about the only thing they have in common is that they wake me up with a terrible feeling attached. Lots of dreams wake me up, but every single one of these does," she looked at him as though she had no more explanation to offer.

"How many have you had?"

"A few. All different."

16

"When did they start?" He asked trying to find some pattern or connection to the cafeteria incident.

"The first one I ever had was when I was twelve. That one was bad," she said with a tone of warning in her voice.

"Do you mind telling me?"

"No. It's not possible for you to think I'm any weirder than you already do, so why not? I woke up in the middle of the night, around 3:30, feeling like I was falling, but I wasn't. I had dreamt that my class—all eighteen of us—went on a field trip. We were on a yellow school bus driving somewhere that seemed up high, like a mountain area. I never knew where we were specifically, but when the class went to get back on the bus, only seven people boarded. One of them was my science teacher, but the students were faceless, random people who I didn't know. The rest of us were just standing on this high cliff. The

17

doors closed and the bus sat there for a few minutes running. The bus number was 113. All of a sudden the bus sped up the road. It went off the cliff head first and caught fire on the way down. Then there was a huge explosion and the seven people inside died. It burned up and there was nothing left of the bus," Toni said staring like she could picture the scene in her head.

"Wow! That would wake me up too. Was there a bus accident the next day?"

She shook her head. "I convinced myself it was a dream and tried to go back to sleep, but couldn't. It really creeped me out, and this was the first time I ever felt that freaked by a dream. I told my mom I had a bad dream when I was leaving for school, but didn't get into it. Later, I told a few friends that I didn't sleep well because of a dream, that it was a field trip where some students died, but I didn't explain how. My friends said that it was just a dream and I didn't bring it up again. Later

18

that day, the nuns called the whole school down to the gym, which was legendary, because it also served as the auditorium, and was probably half the size of a standard gym. It had a tile floor, so falling was frowned upon, and during CYO basketball games, all the players used to get really angry, because to take the ball in from out of bounds, they had to put a leg behind them on the mat that padded the wall, since the stage was set into the gym wall with no room to separate the two at all. Alas, I digress," she looked at Ralph, who was smiling about her commentary.

"Once we got to our `gymatorium' the whole school—all 200 of us—was asked to sit in the folding chairs that Mr. Peacock, our very cool janitor, had set up for us. He rolled out a TV on a cart, plugged it in, and turned on the news. Our principal, Sr. Marie, got on the microphone and told us that we were in for a special treat, because the Challenger Space Shuttle was about to launch. She said that it would be a part of our history, and that this mission was incredibly important since Christa McAuliffe was the first teacher to go into space with the astronauts. Thousands of teachers applied, including our own science teacher, Mrs. Lorenzini, who claimed she would, `give her eye teeth to go up there.' We watched in anticipation, and everyone counted down with mission control. It was one of the coolest things I ever saw. The rockets flared up and raised the shuttle into the blue sky. People were cheering, clapping, waving flags, and all of Christa McAuliffe's family and students were there to see her off. It was so exciting, because we would hear first-hand from an actual teacher, not a textbook, what space is really like. There was a clock in the lower right corner of the TV screen, and at precisely 1:13 into the launch, something went wrong. Parts started coming off of the rocket and shuttle. Then there was a fire, which started streaking through the air upward, until a thunderous explosion, and that was it. What was left fell to the ground like cinders from a fireworks show. The whole gym was silent, even TV for a second. The news cut to a commercial and Sr. Marie turned the TV off. Everyone felt awful. I felt guilty, like I knew and should have said something." She looked at Ralph waiting.

"You have no reason to feel guilty. That launch had been planned for months, and I doubt even if you said something the information would have been received by the proper channels in time, or even taken into consideration for that matter. You were just a twelve-year-old kid. They wouldn't have listened to you anyway," he said with conviction.

"I know that's exactly what would've happened, but I never told anyone the details, and once that happened, it was too late to share. People would've either thought I was psycho or wanted attention. I went home when school was over and watched all the footage over and over to see if there was some clue.

21

The bus was an obvious parallel to the shuttle, but I didn't notice the bus number matched the time of the explosion until I saw it a few times on the news. Same with the seven people, the fact that one of them was my science teacher, and how the bus caught on fire were all identical. She was so sad. She had a big poster of Christa McAuliffe that said, `I touch the future. I teach.' on her wall. I didn't tell anyone about that dream until high school when I would dream like that again," Toni said solemnly.

Ralph got up from the chair he was sitting in and headed for her classroom door. As he turned the handle, he looked at Toni, "It may not seem like it, but that's a gift you got there." He walked through the door and it closed behind him.

22

The Accident

She sat for a moment looking at the multitude of papers she needed to clean off her desk when her eyes drifted toward the clock on the wall, "*This mess will be here tomorrow,*" she said to herself while reaching for her cell phone. She turned off her classroom lights, locked the door, and headed out of the building for the parking lot. As soon as she got settled, she dialed her friend Nina. After three rings she answered, "What's up chica loca? Isn't this early for you?" Nina asked cheerily.

"Yeah. I just left. I'm mentally exhausted," Toni said sounding tired.

"What? Superteach is leaving early, and by that I mean three hours after everyone else left the building," she said sarcastically, one of Nina's purest traits.

"You're not funny," she said flatly.

"Oh, but I am. How many years has it been?" Nina questioned.

"Two."

"Then you got three to go. After that it's adios muchachos!" she said enthusiastically.

"I don't know. I like it here."

"Uh-oh. I'll have to commence severe brainwashing to help you stick to the plan," Nina chuckled.

"The plan you invented," she reminded her.

"You'll thank me in the long run. So what's up witchu? Why are you grumpytone? I know a grumpytone when I hear one, and you're grumpy. Grrr!" she laughed.

"I'm not grumpy. I'm sad. I've been thinking a lot about what happened in the cafeteria, and it just made me think about Bruce," Toni's voice had a heaviness to it.

"Dude, you're not responsible for any of that stuff. Granted it's freaky, but no one got hurt at school. Maybe that's fate's way of telling you that you did a good thing. You didn't have to alert your boss, but you did, and in the end, the kids were safe," Nina said suddenly more serious but keeping her lighthearted way.

"Bruce wasn't that lucky. I warned Bruce, and he still got hurt."

"You warned him about a car accident, not a carnival."

"There's always some element that's different. I never know what it's going to be."

25

"Exactly, so there's no reason for you to beat yourself up about something that you technically had no control over. Besides, you came up on the scene just afterward. You didn't even know what happened until the mad scramble to save him was in progress. What? Were you supposed to glue yourself to his side the whole day and put him in a bubble?" Nina was waiting for an answer.

"No. That day plays over in my head all the time though," she said empty.

"I wasn't anywhere near the scene and still remember the commotion. It's one of those events you never forget. Over two thousand kids outside and you could hear a pin drop. I think that was the spookiest part for me. You were right there and experienced a lot worse. I didn't know him that well, so most of what I felt was through knowing you and what you told me," Nina recalled.

26

"I had been teasing him the whole month before to quit screwing around and date Dina. She and I were always hanging out because she was one of my yearbook editors, and he was constantly coming around to see her. Eventually, I became friends with him. By the end of the year, it was obvious that they should date, and I'm not sure what was holding him back, but two days before the carnival he called me to discuss his romantic plan to ask her out. That night he got all dressed up, doused himself in Polo, because Dina loved the way it smelled on him, picked up a dozen long stemmed red roses, and drove to her house. He rang the doorbell, she answered, he held the roses out, and said, `So I've been thinking about this *us* thing, and I'm way overdue. I can be a little slow sometimes.' They both smiled, he kissed her, and they were official after Dina made a point of reminding him how charming he thought he was and how patient she really was. They called to thank me for encouraging them, and were acting fairly giddy. Seconds

27

later they had their first mini-fight. Dina invited him to be at our carnival booth, and Bruce, as per usual, had already made plans with the guys from the baseball team. I hate baseball! I don't think I've ever watched as much baseball as I did those few years, and I loathed every minute of it," Toni snarled.

"You hate baseball like I hate mushrooms," Nina empathized.

"How you can hate shrooms is beyond me, but yes, it's that bad. Although they agreed to disagree that night and ended on a positive note, they kept they're separate plans for the carnival the next day. I finished up the last few touches really late, and was wired for sound when I got home, so it took me forever to fall asleep. What seemed like moments, but was really a few hours after I did, was the next disturbing dream I would have. I woke up thinking the whole scenario already happened and it was too late. Twenty minutes or so later I figured out that I still had a fighting chance to turn this one around. I dreamt that Bruce was on his way to Dina's to ask her out, like he was in reality hours sooner, except this time, he didn't make it. While he was driving to her house, a tractor trailer hit his Mercury Topaz in the front on the driver's side, crushing his legs under the steering wheel. He was trapped and couldn't free himself. One whole side of the car was missing, but Bruce's car was pinned up against the truck. Emergency vehicles flooded the streets to save him. Firefighters cut him out of the car, and as they removed the last piece of twisted metal that prevented them from reaching him, a lone baseball fell out onto the street and rolled away. I called Bruce as soon as I figured out it hadn't happened yet. He answered right away, because he was still on the phone with Dina. He was too engrossed in his conversation with her to pay attention, told me it was a dream, not to worry about him, and that he was glad he wasn't dead in the dream. I told him it wasn't funny, he should listen to me, and come with us the next day, but he chuckled instead and told me he'd talk to me at the carnival. Since Bruce was never serious about much, I called Dina and warned her. She had the opposite reaction, got totally nervous, and begged him to come with us, but he laughed harder and said we were both paranoid." Toni was silent for a few seconds.

"I think paranoid's your middle name," Nina jested.

"I openly admit that I'm paranoid. Dina tried. She really pleaded for him to come with us, even the next morning when I met Dina at our booth; she seemed as desperate as I was. `Why does he have to be so stubborn?' she said. I didn't calm her down, because I felt like we were doing the right thing trying to change his mind. I asked Dina what made her believe that this incident had the potential of occurring, and I'll never forget it. She said, `You're one of those intuitive people that just knows things, and Bruce is usually up to some mischief, so between the two of you it's not looking good.'

That was the last time that day we laughed. Right at that moment I heard some of my friends screaming that they needed the nurse at the obstacle course. I looked at Dina. Without hesitation, we sprinted up the hill to find a crowd forming larger by the second around Bruce, who was face down in a huge mud puddle motionless. That was one of the scariest images I ever saw. I looked over at Dina. She had panic in her eyes and tears streaming down her face. Two of my friends were volunteer firefighters and argued that he didn't have much time, because they were either going to hurt him if they moved him or he would drown in the muddy puddle. The pair flipped him over as quickly and gently as possible, washed him off with a hose. Bruce was unconscious and didn't seem to be breathing. The student volunteers attended to him faster than the trainer or nurse could even get there. My friends got him to breathe, but they weren't certain how badly he was injured. An ambulance pulled up just outside the field.

Some paramedics got out, talked with the students who helped him for a few minutes, and determined he was too unstable to move. In what felt like an eternal twenty minutes, a medevac chopper landed on the soccer field, where I'd watched him play in the Fall. I had a haunting feeling I may never get the chance to see him play again. There was no noise except for helicopter propellers, which made an eerie sound like those in the beginning of Billy Joel's *Goodnight Saigon*. They loaded Bruce onto the chopper and rushed him to Jeff downtown. Dina pushed her way through the chaos to one of our teachers and cried, 'I'm his girlfriend. Did anyone call Bruce's parents?' I told Dina I'd drive her down there, and our teacher raced toward the building to contact his family. My car was right by the fence, and as I sped away, the dense gathering of people parted so we could pass," Toni remembered.

"I couldn't tell you what was going on until the helicopter showed up, because I was hanging out by the band room. I was the informative one, because once I heard it was Bruce, who I only knew through you, then people started asking me a million questions I didn't have the answers to. It was quiet. I remember that more than anything. For all those people and everything that was going on, it was silent," Nina explained her vantage point.

"It takes about a half hour to get downtown, but we were at the emergency room door in seventeen minutes. We raced into the waiting room and saw his brother and sister, who told us his parents were with him, and they didn't have any information yet. Hours went by and many boxes of tissues later, Bruce's parents emerged from the trauma unit. They told us that he'd fallen into the puddle face first and broke his C five and six vertebrae. He was just waking up, in shock, and a state of spinal trauma. They didn't know how long it would take until the doctors could determine how extensive the ambulatory damage was, that he would be in the hospital for a while, and he needed to rest, but we could go see him because he was asking for us. Dina and I walked into the room slowly and saw a horrific sea of tubes, wires, monitors, and Bruce in a neck stabilizer still with mud on him. Dina burst into tears, grabbed his hand, and stood over him telling him she loved him repeatedly. Since Bruce was never serious, and I'm all about levity in awful situations, I attempted smiles and bad jokes, which luckily he responded to and managed to smile back. He asked me to take care of Dina. I said I'd bring her to visit him every day. She kissed him and told him to feel better. As we turned to leave he said, `Hey Tone, do me a favor? Don't have any more dreams about me ok?' I could feel my heart in my throat, which I promptly choked down, nodded, and told him to stop wrestling crocodiles. We went downtown every day for a year, first to Jeff then to Magee. Dina stopped coming with me about half way through. Said she couldn't stand to see him in that chair, and that it broke her heart every time all over again." Toni was silent.

"Well thank you Debbie Downer for that incredibly sad recap of one of the worst experiences we lived through. Is there a reason you're thinking about miserable events?" Nina pressed.

"I've been pondering a lot lately."

"You do like to ponder. Haven't we determined that you should never be left unattended, especially with your thoughts?" Nina said in a scolding, yet joking tone.

"That's why I called, so I wouldn't get stuck in a bad loop tape of thinking about this," Toni defended herself.

"Think, think, think. You're like my own personal Winnie the Pooh! You were already majoring in enough subjects. Did you really need to add psych to the list? You know I'm all about numbers. They're so much easier! Two plus two is four, or dos y dos son cuatro," she chuckled.

Toni's smile gave way to a laugh, "You're loca. That's why we're friends. I'll catch you mañana chica de hoy."

"Smell ya later!" The call ended, and Toni closed her flip phone that everyone gave her grief about since the technology was old.

"Another day of clean up and then we'll see what next year brings," she thought to herself as she pulled into her driveway and parked her SUV.

The Lottery

While thinking about yet another set of yearbook deadlines and the upcoming international night event, Toni wrestled her mind to sleep. Since there were typically not enough hours in her day, she generally hit the pillow exhausted and was asleep in seconds, but this night she had so many springtime activities and final exams looming in her consciousness detaining her from the four or so hours she was lucky to garner each weeknight. Eventually, her fatigue would prevail and give way to slumber, but her rest was cut short. Less than an hour after she fell asleep she woke up smiling with a clenched fist, as if she was holding on to an object. She muttered senselessly, as she often did in her unconsciousness, and laughed loudly enough until her eyes opened and she was wide awake. She looked at her hand expecting a piece of crumpled paper with numerals on it. Toni reached for a tablet from her night table and clicked a G-2, her favorite disposable pen, to scribble the figures so she wouldn't forget them. *"I have to give these to Darla first thing in the morning. They're important,"* she thought to herself. It had been three years since she encountered one of *those* dreams. This one was urgent, but she didn't seem to know how to feel about it, as there was no imminent danger. She forced herself back to what became a restless night's sleep. A few hours later she readied herself and departed for work a little early. In her jacket pocket, she kept feeling for the paper so she could tell Darla the numbers. She arrived at work and proceeded directly into the guidance office in search of Darla Mela, a young, loud, fun-loving mom, who worked as a secretary. People joked that she shared some personality traits with Roseanna Roseanadana from the old Saturday Night Live skit with Gilda Radnor. When Toni entered the office, Darla was feverishly typing a conference memo.

"Ciao, Darla!" Toni greeted her equally full-blooded Italian friend.

"What's up, Tone? How you doin'?" Darla answered with her trademark South Philly accent.

"I had the weirdest dream last night, and it was all about how I had to get this phone number to you. I don't know who the number belongs to or what it's about, but I got a call in the dream saying it was critical I write this number down and give it to you immediately. The weird thing is, I was only told three digits of the phone number. I had to tell you. Even the dream said it was important." Toni smiled.

"Aw, Tone, that's no joke! You know I play the numbers every night. My dad's retired and he goes every day to play the lottery," she hastily reached for a pen and her own piece of scrap paper.

"I thought you might appreciate knowing about the dream even if it doesn't amount to anything. All I kept hearing was how critical these numbers were to you and that I had to tell you what they were, so here you go." Toni told Darla the three numbers.

"Italians are superstitious, Tone. We pay attention to little things like that. You bet I'll play 'em! I'm gonna call my father right now. He'll be thrilled since they came from a dream. I should go home and look dem numbers up in my dream books. I betcha they mean something. Like I says, 'You can't win if you don't play.' Right?" Darla said very enthusiastically.

"I don't know if it'll mean anything. I just wanted to make sure you knew," Toni shrugged.

"Oh, it means something, Tone. You gotta have faith. It's a sign. It's good luck." Darla nodded and smiled.

"I hope so. Buona fortuna!" Toni said as she turned to leave the office.

"Mille grazie!" Darla boomed as she picked up the phone to call her father.

The rest of Toni's day was fairly uneventful. She taught her classes, graded papers, worked with the yearbook staff, made some calls, and didn't hear anything else about the numbers from the dream. She spent a good amount of time thinking about them and why they might be significant, but couldn't think of anything they related to that would matter. She shared her dream with a few of her colleagues, who were more amused by Darla's reception of the information than intrigued by the dream itself. On her way out Toni stopped in to see her math buddy, Anita, a feisty, pint-sized teacher who she admired very much. The two have a lot in common despite their slight age difference, and Toni wanted to run the numbers by her.

"Hey, chi fa?" Anita greeted.

"Non c'è male," Toni said as she grabbed a chair to sit down.

"What's going on with Darla? She came racing down here a few hours ago to tell me you gave her some numbers and she can't wait to play them?" Anita looked for clarification.

"I guess weird news travels fast too. That's what I was going to tell you. I had another crazy dream where---"

"Wait! Crazy dream like the cafeteria crazy dream?" Anita interrupted.

"Yeah, exactly like that except this one was a phone number that I had to give to Darla because it was really important. The strange thing is there were only three numbers. Way too short for a phone number," Toni raised an eyebrow to indicate she was puzzled.

"You can't ignore that. You just can't ignore that. It has to mean something," Anita said seriously.

"I figured Darla would seek you out. I mean we're pretty limited around here in terms of crazy, superstitious Italians, so it was a matter of time," Toni chuckled.

"You watch. Something's going to happen with those numbers. I don't know what, but something's going to happen with those numbers. Everything happens for a reason. We just don't know what it is yet. Did you tell little mommy?" Anita asked with affection.

"Not yet. I figured I'll tell her and Pop during geriatric meal time, which is rapidly approaching, so I better bolt. Sadly, I knew you'd still be here," Toni yawned.

"Always. There's too much to do and not enough hours in the day. I'm still not done, but I'm leaving. I have choir practice tonight and Mr. Anita's going to want dinner when I get home. I'm not cooking! I love to cook, but I hate figuring out what to make," she said disgusted with the thought.

"Pick up some hoagies on the way home. They're quick and easy," Toni offered.

"Signorina, that's a good idea!" she said elated.

"I don't cook. I eat, so I'm a wealth of knowledge when it comes to procurement of needs."

Anita gathered her purse and satchel full of papers, and the two walked out together.

Toni arrived home and within an hour sleepily plopped on the couch abandoning her typical hyper speed thoughts out of exhaustion. *Jaws*, her first and favorite movie was on TV. She grimaced in drowsiness that the shark didn't prevail in the end, a disappointment she'd had since childhood, which would cause her to always route for the shark. She developed quite an affinity for sharks, especially great whites, courtesy of Benchley and Spielberg's masterpieces. As she drifted off imagining feeding great whites by hand, Toni was abruptly snapped back to reality by a louder than necessary phone ringer she installed for her extremely deaf, but in denial about it, father. "Hello?" she said with 911 urgency still not totally awake, but pretending to be.

"Tone, you won't believe it! We hit! We hit! I sent my dad to play those numbers you gave me this morning and we won! My dad and I played them every which way possible and we won $2500!" yelped an elated Darla, who already had a habit of talking loud enough to nullify hearing aid use.

A stunned Toni laughed, "That's great! I'm glad they meant something. It's about time a dream of mine amounted to a positive outcome. I bet your dad's stoked!" She knew it was his life's dream to hit the lottery, any lottery, just to say he won. Her father wanted the exact same thing. `Must be another South Philly thing,' she thought to herself.

"He's so happy! I've never seen him like this. We owe it all to you, Tone. Thanks so much! You made an old man and his daughter really happy today, and nothin' can take the place a dat. It's like Christmas and his birfday all at once. Anything you need, Tone, you come to me. You got it? Cause I'll never forget dis," said an earnest and sentimental Darla.

"No problem. I'm glad you won and he's happy. Nothing can take the place of that,"

Toni said thinking about how her own father would react.

"I'll see ya tomorrow, Tone! Thanks again and God bless!" an enthusiastic Darla disconnected.

Toni watched the little Kitner boy being eaten on mute while pondering the statistics of what just happened, and thinking about the other dreams that didn't have happy endings when it occurred to her—she never bought herself a ticket.

The Tractor

After three or so dream free years of the disturbing caliber, Toni experienced a series of boring days during the Spring semester when the students were getting ready for state testing. She had been discussing with Claire and Anita how quiet and typical the last few weeks were. Just as she became comfortable with the notion that the calm era may stay, Toni had the most violent dream of her life. She struggled to get out of a deep sleep, which held her paralyzed. She saw one of her student's houses from outside, and her father opening the garage to begin yard work. He prepped a large tractor to cut the lawn. While he was checking the gas tank, he neglected to notice a loose part in the gear shift. Toni could see it and tried to speak but couldn't. She walked closer to the garage, but the father didn't seem to see her. He sat on the tractor, started it up, and drove onto the lawn where he began cutting a large, sloped hill. Toni grew more anxious with every turn the father made.

As he approached the top of the hill on his fifth turn, Toni looked at where the tractor was parked in the garage. She saw two metal parts, a small coil, and a screwdriver on the floor. A sudden panic that the father would be seriously hurt came over her. She turned to chase him off the tractor only to see him force what appeared to be a sticking gear shift at the top of the hill. The tractor stuttered, made a horrible grinding sound, and shook the father off of the tractor in its path downhill. In a matter of seconds, he was sliced up in a bloody wake and killed instantly. As soon as she saw the carnage, Toni was released to consciousness. She sprung from bed with a sore throat from screaming, sweaty, and convinced the ordeal happened. She ran to the bathroom and splashed cold water on her face to collect herself, went back to her bedroom, and looked at the clock. It read 4:01. Recognizing it was a dream, yet still one she had to do something about, Toni thought about her class schedule. It was Jess' father that was so gruesomely slaughtered in the accident, and Toni didn't teach her the next day. She did, however, have Jess' best friend Jules in her fourth period class, so she opted to explain the situation to her and see if Jules knew what study hall she was in so Toni could explain.

A troubled Toni could not find her way back to sleep, and only convinced herself to try since logic would dictate normal people don't cut their grass at 4am on a workday. She tossed and put pillows over her head, but couldn't get the scissored vision of Jess' father out of her head. Toni sought after extra time to sleep almost every day, but this night time was like the slow drip of a leaky faucet. Regardless of enthusiasm or patience, time passed, and Toni was able to leave for school. She was always left to wonder what the people on the receiving end of the information thought. Did they think she was crazy or trying to get attention, or did they truly realize that she was genuinely concerned and attempting to help them? Toni prepped for her classes and seemed to speed teach through her second and third periods, which left the students asking more questions than usual since most of them think she talks too fast anyway. A point she would always return with the possibility that they listened too slowly. The bell denoted the end of third period and Toni was out of the class and down the hall to fourth before the students even exited to the corridor. She dropped her materials on the desk and stood by the door frantically searching for Jess potentially passing in the hallway or Jules walking into class. A few minutes later Jules strolled in with a couple of her friends.

51

"Jules!" an overly excited Toni belted startling the typically reserved, keep to herself Jules. "I have something incredibly important I need to speak with you about." Jules could tell it was serious and walked to toward the desk.

"¿Qué pasa?" Jules said trying to infuse at least some Spanish in an otherwise tense conversation.

"Do you know where Jess is right now? If so, can you go find and retrieve her?" Toni blurted out.

"Sure. Can you tell me what this is all about? Jess isn't in any trouble or anything is she?" Jules asked ready to defend her best friend.

"No. She's fine. I just really need to talk with her immediately. Can you go get her for me? Here's the hall pass," she handed the piece of wood painted with the word baño to her.

"I'll go get her, but you're freaking me out. What's going on? I know how you get and your little Spidey sense is usually right, so should I be alarmed?" pressed Jules in anticipation of something awful to follow.

"I'll tell you the whole story when Jess gets here," Toni's voice was getting louder.

"Please tell me what's going on first!" begged the nervous best friend.

"I had a horrific dream that Jess' dad was killed in a freakish accident, and I think it might be preventable, so I want to explain it to her," Toni said speaking quicker than ever.

"What? Yo, that's creepy! Like a car accident?" Jules asked confused.

"No, a tractor. He was brutally cut up."

"Like a lawn mower? That's disturbing! I'd want to know that if it was my dad. I'll go get her right now." Jules raced out the door.

The two minutes it took on the clock for them to return clicked by like an eternity. "T, what's the deal? You dreamt my dad is going to die? What?" asked a shaken Jess.

"I'm sorry to have to tell you all of this, and I know it seems ridiculous, but I'd rather be cautious and wrong than regretful and right," Toni said like she'd done this before, yet it never got any easier. She told Jess the whole story with Jules by her side.

Mid-sentence Jess raised her voice, "Wait! What day is today?"

"It's Wednesday. Why?" questioned Jules.

"Oh my God! My dad's off today. He said he had extra vacation time that he was going to lose so he took today off, and he was going to cut the lawn!" Jess' eyes opened wide.

"Call him. The phone's there. Dial 9! Call him now before he does it. Go!" yelled a spastic Toni.

Jules flew across the room, dialed Jess' home number, and tossed her the phone. "It's the machine! Dad, it's me. If you get this message do NOT cut the grass! Do you hear me? Whatever you do, don't cut the grass! Don't even go near the tractor. I'll explain later." She hung up the phone. "What do I do?" she asked desperately.

"Does he have a cell phone? Try that," suggested Toni.

"He never turns it on. I don't even think he has the message set up."

"Jess, your mom works at the high school. Call her and tell her to go home," Jules said thinking resourcefully.

Jules dialed the four-digit extension and luckily reached her mother on the second ring.

"Mom, it's me. Yeah, I'm fine. Listen! Go home and stop dad from cutting the grass like now. I know. I'll explain later! I know you're at work! Please just go now. Don't waste any more time! Go now! Please go. I will. Don't let him near the tractor!" Jules didn't seem relieved.

"What's wrong?" Jess asked confused.

"I don't think she's going to go right now. She thinks I'm crazy and kept asking why," Jess said on the brink of tears.

"Keep trying him at home," Jules said sternly, not giving up.

"I'd say explaining would help, but in my experience I really don't think it will. I really hope it's nothing and I'm just being paranoid," Toni said second guessing herself.

"No. You're not. I don't care who thinks I'm crazy. Some people just get stuff like this. They just have a keen sense of intuition, and after that field trip last year, I don't doubt it when you say something feels off," Jules recalled.

"The field trip last Spring? What happened?" Jess pressed.

"We were on our way back to school and we saw an overturned car on the side of the road. The driver looked like no one would stop and tried to flag us down. The bus driver was going to stop, but T told him not to because she had a bad feeling that there was something weird with the dude. She couldn't explain it, and kind of got into an argument with the driver, but we didn't stop. I was even giving her a hard time saying the guy looked like he needed legit help, but she told me it felt wrong. I forgot about it until a few days later when my history teacher was discussing current events, and told me there was a guy on the front page of the paper who posed a disabled vehicle to try and lure people to stop. He murdered three people before they caught him. It was the same guy. The car was in the picture with the license plate. I recognized it from when we were trying to convince the bus driver to stop. That kind of stuff freaks me out. I will never doubt her again. If she thinks something's off, let me tell ya, something's off," Jules attested.

While the girls feverishly dialed Jess' home number to an unanswered ring, her mother had thought better of the call she received from her daughter and drove to their house. As she pulled her gray Volvo into the driveway and ascended the steep curve to the parking pad that paralleled the garage, her heart began to race as she witnessed her husband, already perched on the seat of the tractor, start the ignition. "Stop! Stop! Turn that thing off now!" Jess' mom screamed to no avail. Her father had put the tractor in gear and started out of the garage. "Stop! Stop! Stop!" she cried as she watched him approach the top of the hill. Panic set in her body. All of her muscles tensed as if they were bracing for whatever bad outcome her daughter had warned her about. Thinking quickly in desperation she took off her shoe and threw it at her husband hoping that what he couldn't hear her say over the noisy tractor he would at least feel. The shoe struck him in the upper right shoulder and caused him to jerk forward. He instantly applied the brakes and spun around to see his wife waving her arms wildly in the air. The motor ceased. "Didn't you see me pull in? Or hear me screaming at you?" she scolded him like he was a child.

"What's the matter? You knew I was off today. I'm just cutting the grass!" he snarled back.

"Shut up and get off that thing!" she commanded sternly.

"What?" he asked confused and made a strange face.

"Get off of that tractor!" she said like there would be no other warning and he should heed her word or reap the whirlwind that would ensue.

"Ok. What's wrong?" he asked while shrugging his shoulders and walking toward her and the garage.

"Jess called me very upset while I was at work. She told me not to let you cut the lawn or go near the tractor no matter what. I didn't think anything of it at first, but as I thought, it bothered me. I think she may have saved you from something horrible," his wife said flatly. As she opened the door into the house she could hear the phone ringing. She disarmed the security system and sprinted to the phone, "Hello?"

"You came home from work to stop me from cutting the lawn because Jess told you to?" he sarcastically asked not lowering his voice even though she answered the phone.

"Yes, honey. I got to him just in time. He's fine. I know. I promise. We'll talk about it later. Ok. Love you too. Bye," she hung up the phone relieved. "I'm not sure what all this is about, but I have the sense that I did the right thing. Jess just isn't like that. She seemed so certain," she was partially explaining and talking to herself simultaneously.

"I think you're both crazy! I'm going to put the tractor back in the garage, since apparently it's against the cosmos to cut grass today!" He threw his arms up in surrender.

"No! You can't do that! Just leave it where it is. I promised Jess," she was serious.

"Are you listening to yourself?" his eyes wide open with disbelief.

"Who cares when the lawn gets cut?" she snapped.

"I care! I'm the one that cuts it! I'd rather not waste my day off. This is one of the

61

things I wanted to get done," he barked as he stormed back toward the tractor.

"Don't you go near that tractor!" she warned.

"Or what?" he asked tempting fate. "I'm just getting the keys from the ignition, ok?" asking fake permission. He attempted to remove the key, but it was stuck in the off position. He wiggled it toward the neutral position so it would loosen.

"Leave it alone. Something's obviously wrong with it," shouted his angry wife.

"It's a key. There's nothing wrong with it!" he retorted still struggling with its extraction. A soccer ball whizzed by his face, launched from his disgruntled spouse. "Stop throwing stuff at me! What is with you today?" he turned his head around to argue with her, his hand still fighting with the key.

"You refuse to listen! Our daughter asked you not to do something, something benign, and you won't listen to her. What if I asked you? Would you have listened then?" she tested.

"Oh, so that's what this is about?" he concluded and twisted at the same time. "I would simply like to be told why we are all stressed out about me cutting the lawn? I'm looking for a little clarification here. Didn't think that was too much to ask!" he shouted over his shoulder not noticing the ignition light was now lit solid red.

"Can you stop being ridiculous?" his exhausted spouse questioned.

"I'm being ridiculous?" the father yelled even louder. The tractor bucked forward and started. He whipped his head around in the nick of time to step back from the machine, which seemed to have a mind of its own. The tractor ploughed forward at a faster rate than

63

normal chopping everything in front of it to bits. A metallic clanking sound was growing progressively louder. A trail of oil leaked behind the tractor now obliterating the soccer ball. The sound abruptly stopped and something was expectorated out the side. The tractor rumbled over a rough patch of grass at the top of the hill on the property, and sailed down all the way to the street, where it hit the wooden mailbox, flipped over and shredded bushes, flowers, and the mailbox itself before it sputtered out dead. The two parents stared down the hill in shock. The father investigated the oil trail and then walked to the object it released. Sticking straight up in the grass was a screwdriver, one he had been working on his car with earlier in the week. He rested it on top of the tractor and eventually forgot he left it there. When entering his car, he accidentally knocked the screwdriver into the motor of the tractor. The screwdriver was all chewed up in the handle. He picked it up and remembered using it a few days ago. He turned to his silent wife, "We owe Jess a new soccer ball."

The Fire

The following October Toni was busy with first quarter grades, pep rallies, and Homecoming, like every other Fall. Halloween was the same night as the big rival game this year, and Homecoming was just a week after that. The Phillies won the World Series and Philly decided it was a good idea to have a victory parade on Halloween, which happened to be both the Friday of the grudge match football game and Toni's annual Día de los Muertos fiesta. She was extremely disappointed that her classes would have less than eight students each that day and that red and white would replace orange and black. Her tradition of quesadillas and scary stories would fall upon very few students. Baseball was synonymous with long division in Toni's view, math was not her strong suit.

October held an air of the unusual this year with all that was in the works citywide and locally. Since Toni despised change, anything that would threaten tradition and her typical routine caused immense stress. She was also a superstitious creature, which only added to her angst. Toni never did well on the 13th. She hated the number, thought it unlucky, and wanted nothing to do with it. If it was up to her the world would be excused from everything on the 13th of every month. It was a double negative this year, as the 13th fell on a Monday. Toni never slept well on Sunday nights, because she was always out late running her entertainment business DJing, delivering equipment, taking pictures, or shooting video. Sundays she would sleep late exhausted from her normal weekly rest deprivation. It was an annual vicious cycle from September until June.

The night of the 12th Toni stared at the ceiling in her room contemplating how bad the next day would be. For a few hours she nodded in and out of consciousness, but kept waking to the same image—fire. She couldn't see any details just fire in front of brick. Two hours before Toni had to wake up she fell into a light, restless sleep. She repeatedly saw college textbooks covered in soot and heard her sister's dogs barking as if they were in her room. The obnoxious buzzer of her little, pink Conair alarm clock she bought in the '80s woke her into the reality that the dogs weren't there and it was quiet in the house. Confused as to what the unclear images signified, Toni got ready and went to school. As she walked into her classroom, wary that it was the dreaded 13th, Claire greeted her and followed behind, "You have some serious dark circles under your eyes,

68

chica. You going Goth?" she said attempting to keep up with the lingo.

"It's not Goth anymore. Now it's Emo, and no," smirked a tense Toni.

"You never do well with mornings," Claire stated because she'd seen it before.

"Thank you, Captain Obvious," retorted Toni quickly.

"You should try to get more sleep," suggested a sincere Claire.

"Trying implies failure. Didn't Yoda teach you anything? Do or do not. There is no try. That's like Star Wars 101. You'd never make it in Jedi training. I'll sleep when I'm dead," Toni sounded serious.

"I guess you have a hard time calming your mind down, since you're always going a million miles a second. You're like the Mad Hatter," she quipped.

"I think you mean the rabbit who's late for a very important date. *Alice in Wonderland* creeps me out. It always makes me think of Tom Petty's video for 'Don't Come Around Here No More,'" she corrected.

"How do you do that? Man, you think of things so quickly!" complimented Claire.

"I'm a Generation Xer. That's part of our DNA—spew significant pop cultural references and tie them to iconic masterpieces that teach an important lesson," she explained.

"John Hughes would be proud!" Claire smiled.

"Everything you need to know about life is contained in his work. You can't watch his movies and not have a warm fuzzy by the end. Not to mention writers like Kevin Smith and tons of books, movies, TV shows, comics, and music that emulate the quintessential teen era that have also been successful. I'm actually

70

thinking about making that my topic for my Master's thesis--the hero's journey that Joseph Campbell described. I'm thinking of comparing Luke Skywalker from *Star Wars* to Neo from *The Matrix* to Dorothy from the *Wizard of Oz* to *Don Quijote*," Toni seemed more awake and slightly less paranoid.

"This is for your second Master's, right? Are you stopping after that?" she genuinely asked.

"Nah, there are still way more letters to put after my name," with the intention of pursuing another degree after that.

"I'm surprised you came to school today. I know how much you love the thirteenth," Claire said intrigued by Toni's superstition.

"I should just stay in bed on the thirteenth of every month. In October, there's just something extra potent about it. I guess because it's near Halloween and all things eerie. I loathe the thir---"Toni was interrupted by her cell phone. "Hello?" a nervous Toni asked wondering who would call her that early in the morning. She figured it had to be bad news.

"Tone, it's me! My house is on fire!" screamed her sister, Magenta.

"What? Are you all right? Did you call 911? Are the firemen there?" Toni blurted a series of questions.

"I'm ok. I grabbed the doggies, my books, and my computer, but I'm sitting outside watching my house burn, and Marty's trapped inside!" Her cat had a habit of hiding out in the drop ceiling since the tiles moved.

"I'm on my way. Do NOT go back in the house! Tell the firemen the cat's inside. I'll be there soon," she snapped her phone shut, grabbed her bag, handed Claire a video about Mexican Day of the Dead customs, and said,

"Get me a sub. Magenta's house is on fire and it's the thirteenth! I saw it last night!" Toni took off down the hallway.

Twenty minutes later Toni raced up to her sister's town home, jolted the car in park, and hurried to negotiate the maelstrom of confusion happening all around her. "Are you all right?" she asked in a panic.

"I'm fine. I'm glad I had a few minutes before it got to my house," Magenta said while staring at the hose flooding the flames.

"What happened? When did it start? Where are the doggies?" Toni continued her line of questioning from the phone call.

"Mandy and Molly are in my truck behind us with everything I could grab. It started early this morning around 6:30. I was asleep and I heard someone pounding on my door downstairs. The doggies started barking so I knew something was up. I went downstairs as fast as I could to answer the door, and the neighbors were yelling 'Our house is on fire!' I opened the door to one of the guys standing there saying that sparks just started flying out of the electrical socket. An electrical fire caught soon after in their upstairs room, so they grabbed what they could, ran downstairs, and called the fire department on the way out the door. I knew I only had a few minutes, so I ran back upstairs, threw on some clothes, took my books, laptop, and leashes. The dogs followed me downstairs barking. I dumped everything by the door and went looking for Marty, because I knew he would be in the ceiling. Calling to him didn't work, treats didn't work, and before I could coax him to come down, the firefighters were coming through the door instructing me to leave because the fire was about to burn through. Just as he said it, I could smell that nasty charred stench. They walked in with axes and told me to move my truck across the parking lot to the visitors' spaces. I took everything I could carry with the dogs, loaded

74

my truck, and moved it over here. I've been watching them since I talked to you. I'm really worried about Marty," there was sadness in her voice.

"First of all, cats have nine lives, and your cat most likely has triple that because he plots world domination daily, so he will find a way to survive. Don't stress over the cat. Animals have instincts. He will hide somewhere, and it looks like the firefighters have the situation under control. The flames are going down. Call Mom and Pop because they'll freak out if Joe Cool hears it on the scanner and tells them first," Toni cautioned their volunteer fire fighting brother would hear the dispatch call. "While you're at it you better tell Vicky and Renée," Toni and Magenta's other sister and niece respectively, also not known for remaining calm in a crisis.

"Good point. I'll go call them from inside the truck. It'll be quieter and Pop can't hear anyway," Magenta got in her truck to call the rest of the family.

Toni stared at every inch of the house like she was watching an instant replay from her dream. The brick front covered in flames, the dogs barking uncontrollably, soot covered belongings everywhere, and the foul odor of burned objects. She felt a distinct unsettling feeling that something was unresolved, *"must be the cat,"* she thought to herself, *"or the fact that this lousy number always haunts me."* She looked at her watch. It was 8:13. She shook as if to rid herself of something clinging to her that she no longer wanted.

Magenta exited the truck and stood next to Toni, "Check and check. Everyone now has something to talk about. Pop's already moving stuff around in Zen so I can temporarily move in while my house gets repaired. There's a lot of stuff in Zen though," referring to one of the spare rooms in the house their father built.

"That's true. I guess Zen isn't very Zen. I blame *Rocky Horror*. Your stellar spatially related self will have that room looking all Feng Shui in no time!" Toni was extremely weak in determining measurements, directions, and most geometrical puzzles.

A few hours passed when the firefighters declared the site safe to re-enter. Although her neighbor's house took the brunt of the damage, Magenta's house looked like an axe murderer had run through it on a rampage. The firefighters had to hack into the walls at various points to ensure the fire didn't burn through. There was an incredibly overwhelming scent of scorched brick and all of the contents of her house smelled like smoldering smoke.

"Everything in here will have to be removed and treated and a specialized cleaning team will take care of the house itself. The whole process takes about two months, but it is covered under your home owner's insurance.

77

Do you have a place to stay?" asked one of the helpful firefighters.

"Yes. I'm going to my parents' house. Thank you so much for everything. Did you see my cat?" Magenta asked nervously.

"We didn't see him, although they tend to hide from fire. Put a bowl of water at the edge of the ceiling where he hangs out and call to him. He will be thirsty, so he will surface," suggested the fireman like he's seen this quite often.

"Thanks again. I'll go do that right now," Magenta ran into the house, filled a bowl with water, and began calling to Marty. After a few minutes, a faint "Meow" came from the darkness in the ceiling. Seconds later a soot covered orange and white Marty emerged to lap up the water. Magenta took him down after a long drink and scooped him into his cat carrier for the trip home. She immediately called the groomer to get him cleaned.

"I still can't believe the house was on fire," Magenta remarked while getting into her truck.

"I'm glad it wasn't as awful as it could've been. Today is the thirteenth," Toni seemed disconnected.

"That date never used to bother me. I'm thrilled Marty's all right. What's with you? Seems like you're hung up on something," she looked at her sister inquisitively.

"I didn't want to tell you this before, but I guess it's safe now. I dreamed this whole thing last night. Couldn't sleep because it kept waking me up. Maybe if I had called you when I woke up---"

"Nope!" Magenta cut her off. "Put Big eye away!" she commanded her sister to release the thought of guilt from her typically raised eyebrow, who had its own name because it was prevalent so often. "Don't even start thinking like that. It was a freak thing, and you had no way to know that it would really happen. Everyone's fine and that's all that matters. In my haste I only thought to take my text books, laptop, and the dogs, which is funny because you had to twist my arm to finish my degree and my job has always overworked and underpaid me. I didn't even think to get some of my clothes, puzzles, or pictures!" she said now laughing. Toni smiled and chuckled with her, but couldn't let go of the dream stuck in her mind.

Why did this happen? Why did some dreams simply remain dreams and every so often one would turn into some type of reality? Was there a pattern to them? Were they signs or warnings? More importantly, were there any she had dismissed in the past that didn't surface yet? These questions plagued her, and she still didn't have any answers.

The Salute

The next few years were eventful dream free, and although Toni had some paranoid moments, she enjoyed the typical and the boring. Routines suited her nicely and she was thankful for them. In the midst of prepping for another approaching holiday season, Toni stayed late grading papers at school so she could meet up with the Advent calendar delivery that the world language club always sold. The vendor called her an hour later than he should have been there and said his truck had broken down at the Outback Steakhouse about a mile away, and asked if she could meet him there. She agreed and began packing up when her phone rang. It was one of her employees. "Hey Tone! Tim, Wade, and I just got finished a game of football and are pretty hungry, so we were gonna get dinner. Do you wanna come with?" asked the familiar voice on the phone.

"That's funny, Sal. As my luck would have it, the delivery guy I'm supposed to meet just called saying his truck broke down in front of Outback, so if you guys are cool with going there, I'll meet up with you and I can kill two birds with one stone. Sound good?" she asked with total confidence that they would oblige.

"Sounds Gucci! See you in a few!" said an enthusiastic Sal.

Toni drove to the nearby shopping center and saw the distressed truck with an equally distressed driver. "Is a tow truck coming for you?" she asked as she signed for the order.

82

"Yeah, but you know how it is. The guy said over an hour wait, but the company always makes them say that. At least it's cold outside so the chocolate won't melt," the driver said optimistically as he loaded the boxes into Toni's truck.

"True. It could be worse," she said while locking her vehicle.

"It can always be worse. People sometimes forget that when dealing with a smaller problem. When something terrible happens, it makes you appreciate the little upsets in life," he said profoundly.

"Can't argue with that philosophy. I'm glad you have a tow truck on the way. Have a great Christmas!" Toni smiled and walked into the restaurant to have one of her favorite meals with some of her favorite people.

As she entered she couldn't help notice a table in the back of three mud covered, athletic guys barking, "Yo Boss! Back here!" She took off her trench coat and sat down.

"You guys look like you were wrestling pigs! Thanks for getting cleaned up first. I really appreciate being seen in public with you looking like this," Toni said in her usual sarcastic way.

"Are you saying you're ashamed of us?" quipped an also typically sarcastic Tim.

"Never," she smiled.

"What do we have this weekend?" inquired Wade, who thought himself the least capable of all her employees.

"Yeah, how many gigs?" Sal asked.

"Just one this weekend. A sweet sixteen right up the street for a set of twin girls. Only sound and lights. Pretty standard," Toni explained.

"That's easy," said a confident Tim. "Tomorrow night?" he asked remembering it was Thursday.

"Sí, Señor! Mañana noche."

"You're lucky I even remember what that means. Too much science to learn. Getting ready for my engineering classes. Had to bail on the español," said an unregretful Tim as if that was the logical solution so therefore it must be the correct one.

"That's ok, Tim. We can't all be perfect. When you need your designs and patents translated, we'll all be here for you," Toni said firmly joking with a smile on her face.

"Who's doing the gig?" Wade looked at his phone to check his busy social schedule.

"I was going to send Dante and Sal," referring to the only one of that group not present.

"Tomorrow's actually clear for all of us, so we can all go," offered Tim.

"Four of you to spin a basic sweet sixteen? Are you guys bored?" she questioned.

"They should consider themselves lucky that four of the best-looking guys with mucho talent would honor them with their presence," Tim said facetiously.

"Nice. I'll make sure to tell them," Toni said flatly.

"You should also consider yourself lucky that you have a big group of awesome, responsible guys who are excellent disc jockeys, loyal, and love you," Sal said insisting.

"Don't forget honest, intelligent, and have good families with normal parents!" Wade added.

"You do have some specific criteria to make up a decent worker, and lucky you, we fit them all," said a snarky Tim.

"You guys are awesome and so are your families, and you're all so modest too. I think that's your best quality," Toni dished back to them.

"When's company dinner?" Tim asked anxiously.

"The twenty-second. Everyone will be home then."

"Don't worry, Tim. There will be plenty of food for you to eat," Sal joked about Tim's voracious appetite.

"Wade, would you do me a favor while we are waiting on the check?" Toni asked like she just remembered something.

"Sure. What?"

"Can you run next door to the Acme and get a six pack of Gatorade? My brother's been sick with a bad cold for a few days. The doctor said to keep him hydrated and that would be good to give him," she handed him some money and Wade left for the store. Toni looked at her watch. "It's nine o'clock already?" she seemed surprised.

"It's amazing to us that you're still shocked when it's later than you think. You're never on time for anything, because you function on `Toni Time.'" Tim laughed.

"I'm on time for work every day!" Toni barked.

"Yeah, only because you're up all night!" Sal snickered.

"I feel like someone's stealing my time particles," Toni insisted.

"You're in time denial," Tim argued.

88

"That's as bad as you refusing to believe that you drive faster when a song you like comes on the radio," Sal chuckled. Wade walked back in amongst the laughter.

"I put the drinks in your car. What'd I miss? I could hear you guys from out there," he looked at them in anticipation of a story.

"We were just telling Toni that she's in denial about being late all the time and drives faster when she likes the music," Tim stated like a text book fact.

"That's not new news. I don't think she's ever been on time for anything—at least not without our help. It's a team effort, and as for driving, car singing is a clear sign that the gas pedal's on the floor," Wade added referencing her above average vocal capabilities.

"That's it! I'm leaving!" Toni smiled as she got up to put her coat on. "I realize it's national pick on Toni hour, but I have to get home—still have a million things to do." She hugged them all and drove home. On the way Coldplay's newest song came on the radio. Toni found herself singing *"who would ever want to be king?"* and arrived home much faster than she thought she would. Maybe there was something to the guys' theory.

She unlocked the door and walked in with her hands full to the sound of her brother snoring loudly in his room off to the left. He was asleep in his recliner. She put her things down, greeted her mother, and explained the Gatorade was on the table for her brother. Toni had several messages on her phone she needed to return, but wanted to get cleaned up first, so she headed into her room texting along the way. She emptied her pockets, grabbed her robe, and turned on the shower when suddenly she heard a loud thump on the ground from the other end of the house. She turned off the water and hurried to see what it was. As she

90

got to the kitchen her mother yelled, "Rock just fell over!"

"He probably just fell out of his chair," Toni reassured her mother thinking her narcoleptic brother had a bad habit of falling forward while sleeping. She ran in the room and turned on the light to find the large man face first on the floor. "Rock, get up! You ok?" she asked as she knelt beside him on the floor, his chair in the way. "Rock, come on. Talk to me!" she began to panic as she noticed his head was hanging forward. As she reached to pull his head up Toni could feel that her brother's face was ice cold. "Rock! Oh, no! Don't do this to me! You can't leave me like this!" she was talking to him now fearing the worst. "You're supposed to help me take care of them. This isn't the plan!" she said referring to the agreement they had to assist their aging parents. "Mom, dial 911 right now! Rock's not breathing! He's blue and cold," she shouted from his room.

Her mother, hysterical, grabbed the phone frantically obeying the command. "They'll all be here any minute," she yelled from the other room.

Toni's brother was a volunteer fireman for thirty-five years. Everyone from Station 51 would arrive faster than lightning. Operating on pure adrenaline, Toni threw the recliner out of the way and flipped her brother onto his back. She attempted CPR, but to no avail. She pounded on his chest, begging for him to breathe, but his open eyes and motionless body told a different story than the one she wanted to hear. "This can't be happening. It just can't!" Toni said to herself.

"What happened? What's wrong with him?" her mother pressed as if there was going to be a different answer than a few moments ago.

"Mom, he's gone. I'm trying, but he's not responding," Toni said solemnly.

"What do you mean?" her mother asked as if not understanding the words.

"He's gone. He was cold when I found him and his eyes were open. He must've passed in his sleep," Toni said hearing the reality spoken for the first time.

Toni's father burst into the room, awakened from the commotion, and aggravated that his immense hearing deficiencies prevented him from being on the scene sooner. "What happened?" he asked confused.

"Rocky fell and now he's not breathing," his wife said detached from emotion.

"How long has he been out?" his father raced to his side placing his son's arms over his head trying to clear an airway.

A loud bang on the nearby door signaled the fleet of emergency vehicles

93

flooding the driveway and street. "It's Station 51. We're here for Rocco," the deep, authoritative voice said clearly from outside. Toni's mother opened the door recapping the chain of events leading to their arrival.

"Pop, he's gone. I did CPR. He was cold when I found him," Toni explained to her father, who was bewildered.

"We'll take it from here. Please step out so we can best help Rocco," the EMT Captain firmly requested.

Toni switched off her emotions in an effort to accomplish all the impending tasks that were speeding her way. She quickly remembered that in an emergency situation delegating to a specific person is much more effective than just suggesting what had to be done. She looked at her father and said, "Pop, go open up the front door and move the piano, because they're going to need the space to take him out."

94

"Mom, call Magenta. She's been sick with a cold and is probably wasted on Nyquil, so make sure you actually wake her up. Then call Vicky and Renée. Vick's most likely with Dave on their way back from the policeman's holiday ball," Toni instructed as if she was in her classroom reviewing the day's agenda. "I'll call the rectory, *and the undertaker*," she said out loud then thought to herself because it was too harsh of a reality for her mother to yet comprehend.

With a sea of background noise rendered by twenty emergency professionals scurrying throughout the house, Toni made her calls. As she closed her flip phone she heard the side door open. A speechless and confused Renée walked in trying to put the pieces together. "What's going on? Because there's no way what everyone is saying is true," she stated in blatant denial.

95

"He was gone when I got to him. He was blue," Toni said flatly from the zone she put herself in at the onset of the situation.

"Tone, that just can't be!" Renée said sharply.

From a faint distance Toni's mother sounded insistent, "Run the test. Then we'll see what's really going on."

The EMT complied with the request out of respect for the inquirer with no expectations of a change in condition. "Mom, that test isn't going to do anything," Toni said gently.

"It'll show his heartbeat even if it's real faint," she said hopefully.

"It can't hurt to run the EKG. It'll make her feel better knowing for sure," Renée said still teetering on the brink of acceptance.

The test result was a pure flatline with no surprise to anyone except Toni's mother.

"Maybe if they run it again?" her mother suggested.

"Mom-mom, he passed away," Renée walked to her side to comfort her.

A few seconds later a sniffling, choking Magenta came through the door saying that there were so many emergency vehicles in the street she had to park at the end of the cul de sac. "There's no way. I just talked to him yesterday. We were talking about the fact that we both had bad colds. Did he just pass out?" she asked as if there would be some type of mystery solved revealing her brother was still alive.

"They just did an EKG," Renée shook her head.

"Seriously? What happened?" Magenta looked around for anyone willing to answer.

"They think it was an embolism," Toni repeated what she overheard the emergency personnel saying. "That's why he was blue."

The door sprung open to a hysterical Vicky and a very somber Dave, Vicky's incredibly calm, sweet, police officer husband. "Where's Rocky?" she sniffed trying to breathe and cry at the same time. "I want to see him!" she demanded pushing past a few firefighters.

"Vick, they did an EKG. He must've passed in his sleep," Magenta tried to offer a reasonable explanation.

"I want to see the results! Did anybody try CPR?" she argued.

"Toni did, but he was already cold," Renée said to her mother.

The next hour was a blur of the priest arriving to administer last rites, emergency personnel moving equipment in and out of the house, and the undertaker's arrival. His family

98

went to school with all of Toni's. The pacing family and foot traffic of the multitude of professionals strewn about the house mimicked the holiday bustle occurring in everyone's hometown, or so the slogan says of the small, yet popular Philadelphia suburb. The surreal set in when the voice from the other room said, "We are going to take him out now."

"If there are any personal items that you'd like to remove, you should do so now," instructed the solemn undertaker.

Toni walked in to her brother's room, knelt beside him to remove his watch, ring, and bracelet. She placed them on the bureau and kissed him goodbye on the cheek. "You'll always be my Pebble," she smiled remembering their many inside jokes. The nickname she gave him made light of his robust stature. Toni always said there was just more of him to love. It occurred to her upon her exit that was the first time it was quiet in his room for several hours. She struggled with a fleeting thought,

99

but couldn't wrap her head around what it was since her thoughts were interrupted by the undertaker's voice in the kitchen.

"It's ok. You'll see him tomorrow," he consoled Toni's mother and father.

The family moved to the parlor to clear the way for the wall of firefighters who squeezed through the doorway into the kitchen navigating a tough turn with the gurney. As they wheeled her motionless brother into the parlor, where Toni's whole family was standing, all the firefighters offered condolences then walked outside. They stood shoulder to shoulder along the front walkway forming an honor guard. The firefighters saluted their fallen brother as he was taken past each one. Toni's family watched from the bay window inside and were grief stricken.

Renée grabbed for Toni's arm abruptly, "You said this would happen. I remember this. This exact scene. I was a teenager when you told me you dreamt this. It's the front door, all the people in uniform saluting, and Rocky being removed on a gurney and everything!" she said suddenly recalling a macabre rendition of a dream Toni had shared over a decade ago.

"I was hoping it wouldn't end like I saw it, nor did I think you'd remember. You're the only one I told about that," Toni said quietly wishing the image hadn't been galvanized in her memory forever. "I never knew what made me dream that, and it haunted me. I was paranoid that something bad would happen for weeks. Once some time went by, I thought that it would be ok and it was a fluke. Apparently, I was wrong."

"Did you ever tell Rock?" Renée asked.

"No. I figured knowing would only make him paranoid too, although he wasn't like that," Toni rationalized.

"There was nothing you could've done," Renée assured.

"That's the worst part."

A few weeks went by and a darkened set of holidays swallowed Toni's family. Everyone took some time off to heal and recover much needed rest. Toni was exhausted, but her sleep was plagued by nightmares. She couldn't believe that one of her dreams from so many years before would actually lead to the loss of her brother. She poured over the details recounting the story to her closest friends trying to make sense of the bizarre. One night during her holiday break she fell asleep rather late thinking about all the dreams she had that transferred into reality. There never seemed to be a pattern to them or reason for them. That night Toni dreamt of her brother. He was sitting at the kitchen table in one of his many blue shirts, since he was color blind and blue was one of the few colors he could clearly see. He looked up at her from his crossword puzzle, which was part of his daily routine, and with his notorious Cheshire cat grin he said, "I'm ok. Don't worry about me. Aren't you forgetting something?" With that Toni sprung up from bed out of a deep sleep. She was seized by the reality that one of those infamous seven dreams had never been a dream at all.

Acknowledgments

I would like to thank Laura Petrini for creating the cover design. Her melding of the abstract with elements of the tangible is incredible. She is a true artist, fashioning the visual component to complement my words.

From encouragement to providing me with consistent confidence, Bill Straub, Jr. saw me through the creative process so my life's dream could become a reality.

I have been writing as long as I can remember. To the point where I would get frustrated at age three because I did not yet know how to spell the vocabulary I was using, so a gigantic thank you to my family for always taking the time to answer my questions, spell for me, read my work, and constantly encourage me. From my fledgling beginnings on a magnetic letterboard, you have always been there helping to shape the very fabric of the stories I write.

I sincerely thank all of my friends for the time spent helping me plot my next move, assist me with my analysis paralysis, offer constructive feedback, and provide the characters and framework for my stories to unfold. You are such a significant part of my life and have shaped my creativity as much as my family.

None of my talents would have ever been sharpened or utilized without the influence of my teachers. You are a phenomenal set of individuals, who always suggested I keep writing, and gave me the skills to move forward to pursue my dreams. The lessons you taught me are way more than information, rather a way of life, secured in my actions forever.

To all of my family, friends, and teachers who helped in any way big or small to make this endeavor happen, know that you are appreciated, loved, and respected more than any words can ever do justice. You are all an irreplaceable part of my life, have molded the wordsmith I have become, and I am forever grateful.

www.ingramcontent.com/pod-product-compliance
Lightning Source LLC
Chambersburg PA
CBHW071408170626
46811CB00003B/1310